For Bryan, Miriam, and Josephine — P.G.

For Ruby and Harvey — J.B.

First published in the United States in 2019 by
Eerdmans Books for Young Readers,
an imprint of Wm. B. Eerdmans Publishing Co.
4035 Park East Court SE, Grand Rapids, Michigan 49546
www.eerdmans.com/youngreaders

Text © 2017 Patrick Guest
Illustrations © 2017 Jonathan Bentley
First published in Australia by Little Hare Books (an imprint of Hardie Grant Egmont) in 2017

Manufactured in China

28 27 26 25 24 23 22 21 20 19   1 2 3 4 5 6 7 8 9

Library of Congress Cataloging-in-Publication Data

Names: Guest, Patrick, author. | Bentley, Jonathan, illustrator.
Title: The second sky / by Patrick Guest ; illustrated by Jonathan Bentley.
Description: Grand Rapids MI : Eerdmans Books for Young Readers, 2019. |
  Summary: From the moment he is hatched, Gilbert the penguin dreams of
  flying one day and, despite being discouraged by family members, finally
  finds a way to do just that.
Identifiers: LCCN 2018025857 | ISBN 9780802855206
Subjects: | CYAC: Penguins—Fiction. | Flight—Fiction. | Determination
  (Personality trait)—Fiction.
Classification: LCC PZ7.1G8 Sec 2019 | DDC [E]—dc23 LC record available at
https://lccn.loc.gov/2018025857

The Second Sky

Written by **Patrick Guest**

Illustrated by **Jonathan Bentley**

Eerdmans Books for Young Readers

Grand Rapids, Michigan

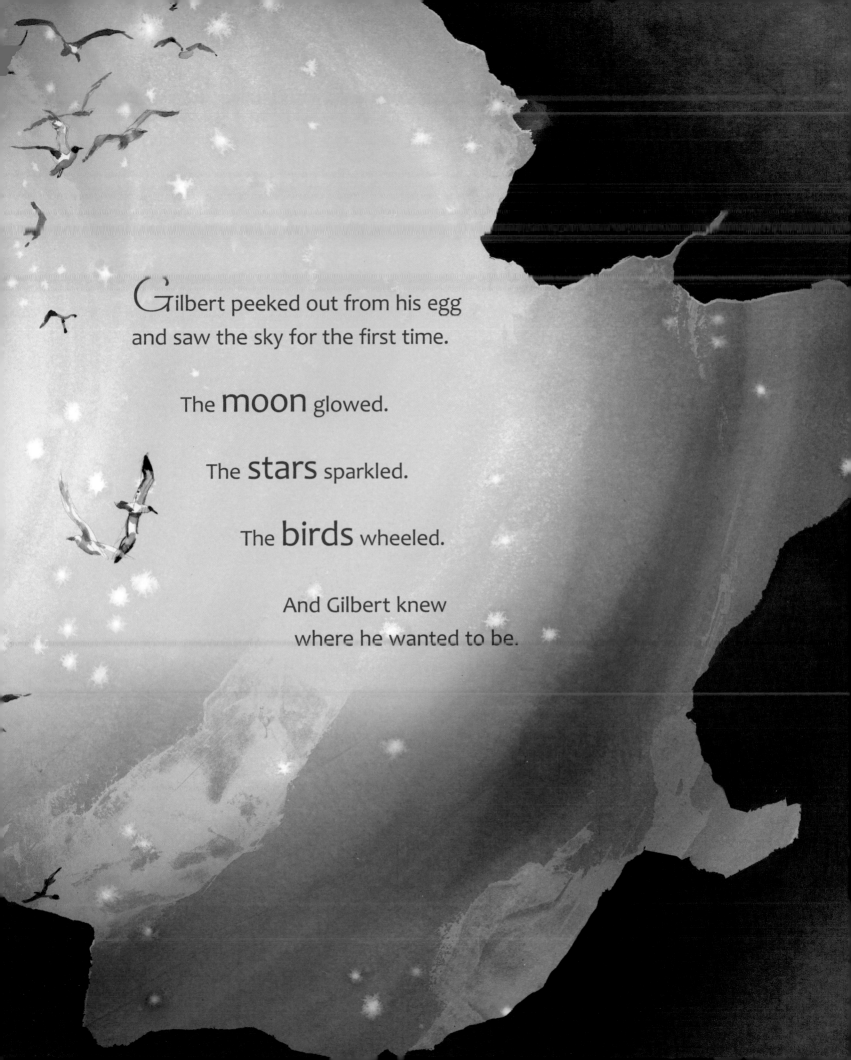

Gilbert peeked out from his egg
and saw the sky for the first time.

The **moon** glowed.

The **stars** sparkled.

The **birds** wheeled.

And Gilbert knew
where he wanted to be.

Up

Up

Up

with the storm petrels,

the shearwaters,

and the wandering albatross.

But Gilbert had big clumsy feet
and small fluffy wings.

He flapped and flapped,
but instead of flying . . .

he fell on his face,

his back,

and his bottom.

"I just need a few more feathers," he told himself.

Gilbert's feathers grew,
and he learned to waddle.

"Now I can do it," thought Gilbert.

He waddled
and flapped,
waddled
and flapped.

But instead of flying . . .

he slipped on the ice,
      tripped on the rocks, and
            stumbled over his sleeping family.

"Give it up, Gilbert," said Uncle Crabstick.

"You're a penguin, not a goose," said Aunt Anchovy.

But Gilbert didn't give up.

He knew if he kept trying, he would find a way to fly.

One day the wandering albatross came gliding across the sky.
The albatross tucked its wings and did a perfect dive.

Then it spread its wings

and *soared.*

It didn't flap once.

"I've been flapping too hard," thought Gilbert.
"I just need to spread my wings and soar."

The albatross glided away on the wind.
Gilbert followed, clambering over rocks and ice.

He waddled

Up

Up

Up

through wind and snow
until he reached the top . . .

. . . and saw the whole world spread out below.

The albatross soared away,
over the sparkling ocean.

"Wait for me," cried Gilbert. "Watch me soar!"

Gilbert spread his wings

and jumped . . .

Down

Down

Down

slipping

spinning

stumbling

tumbling . . .

. . . until he splashed into the sea.

Gilbert tumbled,

bubbled,

and sank.

When he opened his eyes, he saw . . .

stars,

moons,

and clouds.

He sank deeper and saw
floating forests,
swaying gardens,
and mighty mountaintops.

Gilbert tucked his wings
and did a perfect dive.

Then he spread his wings . . .

and *flew.*